The Darwin
Expedition

DISCARD

YA FIC Tulls

Tullson, D.
The Darwin expedition.

PRICE: $9.95 (3559/cl   )

DISCARD

The Darwin
Expedition

Diane Tullson

orca soundings

Orca Book Publishers

Copyright © Diane Tullson 2007

All rights reserved. No part of this publication may be reproduced
or transmitted in any form or by any means, electronic or mechanical,
including photocopying, recording or by any information storage
and retrieval system now known or to be invented, without
permission in writing from the publisher.

Library and Archives Canada Cataloguing in Publication

Tullson, Diane, 1958-
The Darwin expedition / written by Diane Tullson.

(Orca soundings)
ISBN 978-1-55143-678-4 (bound).--ISBN 978-1-55143-676-0 (pbk.)

I. Title. II. Series.

PS8589.U6055D37 2007   jC813'.6   C2006-906611-6

Summary: Following an accident on a remote logging road, Liam and Tej
must call on all their resources to survive the elements and escape
the bear that is following them.

First published in the United States, 2007
Library of Congress Control Number: 2006938694

Orca Book Publishers gratefully acknowledges the support for its publishing
programs provided by the following agencies: the Government of Canada
through the Book Publishing Industry Development Program and the Canada
Council for the Arts, and the Province of British Columbia through the BC
Arts Council and the Book Publishing Tax Credit.

Cover design: Doug McCaffry
Cover photography: Getty Images

Orca Book Publishers
PO Box 5626, Station B
Victoria, BC Canada
V8R 6S4

Orca Book Publishers
PO Box 468
Custer, WA USA
98240-0468

www.orcabook.com

Printed and bound in Canada.
Printed on 100% PCW recycled paper.

010 09 08 07 • 5 4 3 2 1

Acknowledgments

Thanks to Andrew Wooldridge at Orca Book Publishers for having the right words, and to Shelley Hrdlitschka and Kim Denman, always, for their help with the manuscript.

To R.J. and R.J., with love.

Chapter One

Rain is a sheet of water on the windshield of the pickup truck. Lead gray, the sky appears in brief arcs as the wipers slam back and forth. The forestry road clings to an old avalanche slope, and the roadbed is under what must be a foot of mud. Tej's truck wheels spin and the side windows disappear in a spray of mud. Tej white-knuckles the steering wheel.

"Might be too early in the spring to be on this road, Tej."

"We're almost through," he says, his teeth clenched.

"We could turn around."

Tej throws me a look. "We'd waste hours going back, Liam. We do not want to do that."

Through the mud on his side window I peer down at the stump-strewn slope. The truck fishtails, and suddenly I'm getting a good view of that downhill run.

"You're too close to the edge!"

Tej cranks the steering wheel. Plumes of mud plaster the side of the truck. I feel the back end slew, then drop, as a wheel catches the crumbling shoulder. I'm pushed into the seat, like I'm in a dentist's chair that's tilted. Tej mats the accelerator. The engine whines as the back wheels start to spin. Then the truck lurches backward. I cram my foot against the floorboards, as if that will make the truck hold the road. Tej mutters a curse and the wheels grab, and then they slip again. The truck tips and I lean toward Tej, who is flattened against his side window. We're both swearing now. As the truck starts to roll, Tej's Coke can leaves the cup-holder and hangs in the air an instant before erupting on the dash. Coke runs up the inside of the windshield, and then it streams sideways as we continue to roll.

My teeth slam against my tongue and I taste blood. My shoulder and then my head crack against the side window. Old snow in the ditch swipes the side window and fills it with white. Then I see trees, and sky, and I know we're going over again. That's when I close my eyes.

I don't know how many times we flip, but when we stop, we're suspended upside down in our seat belts. At some point the air bags blew and now droop from the dash. The air feels dense and it's too quiet. I take a careful breath and wait—for the truck to roll again or careen down the mountain, but it doesn't. We're stopped. I heave open the door, and then I push up on one hand against the headliner of the truck, easing the pressure off the seat belt so I can unbuckle it. I tuck my head and roll. It isn't pretty, but I manage to get out of the truck.

My legs liquefy, and I grab the door to steady myself. The truck's front end is jammed solidly against a three-foot tree stump. Good thing, because otherwise we'd be tinfoil at the bottom of the mountain. I stumble around the steaming undercarriage and haul open Tej's door.

His hair is hanging in black spines and his dark eyes are the size of quarters. He's scrabbling with the seat-belt buckle.

"My truck."

"I'm fine, thanks for asking."

Tej gets his buckle undone, and for a second I think about letting him drop on his head. But I pull him from the truck. He wobbles a bit, and then he stands, looking at the truck, at the crumpled steel and the twisted bumper, at the tailgate plowed upside down in the mud.

"Wrecked," he says. "Totally fubar."

I wait for Tej to say something more but he is silent. His eyes are wide open, staring. I shuffle my feet. "You can fix it."

Tej gives himself a shake. "Not here, obviously. We need a tow truck." He yanks his hood up on his blue rain jacket and brushes the hair out of his eyes. After a minute he fishes his phone out of his pocket, opens it and then closes it again. He doesn't have to tell me: There's no service this far into the bush.

The daylight is almost gone. I say, "Maybe we can get a ride out on a logging truck. We could come back tomorrow to get the truck."

"We were on this road most of the afternoon and didn't see a truck. Something tells me we won't see one anytime soon, not with this rain, not even if they use this road anymore."

It was Tej's idea to take the old logging road. Like he can read my mind, he says, "We could have waited the entire long weekend for them to clear the accident off the main highway." He shoves a duffel bag under the truck out of the rain. Our gear was in the bed of the pickup. Tej's snowboard is scattered in pieces. I can't

13

even see mine. Rain is running down my neck.

"Maybe they'll send someone."

"Who? Our parents?" Tej kicks a sleeping bag under the truck. "Our parents think we're on the highway to Whistler."

"I mean when we don't call. They'll get worried and start looking for us."

Tej shakes his head. "I never call. My parents expect that I'll be okay or that I'll deal with it."

"I call. Sometimes a few days late, but I always call."

"Well, I'm not sitting here for a few days waiting for an imaginary rescue."

Chapter Two

Tej reaches into the truck and grabs a road map from the overhead console, only now it's on the floor, of course. Rain drills the map as he unfolds it. As he studies the map, his eyebrows knot.

"So?"

He folds the map. "If we stay on the forestry road, we can walk out in a couple of days."

My tongue is sore where I bit it and I

chomp it again. "Walk? For a couple of days?"

"Or we can go cross-country. It won't take more than a day, max." He points with his thumb down the mountain. "We'll drop down over the next ridge and hook up with the main road. Then we hitch a ride into town." He pushes the rest of the gear under the truck and scrambles in after it. "We'll leave in the morning."

I watch his feet disappear under the truck. "How do you know which way to go?"

His voice is muffled. "The forestry road runs east of the main highway. We walk west."

"You don't think it's a bit more complicated than that?"

I hear Tej crack a Coke, then a spraying sound, then Tej curses. I guess the Coke is a bit shaken up. I stick my head under the truck to find Tej wiping his hands on my sleeping bag. I crawl in and grab it from him. Under the truck the rain pings like we're in an oil drum, but it's dry.

Reasonably dry. Tej has taken the most sheltered spot, next to the tailgate; I'm sitting in a small stream of rainwater that runs under the bed of the truck.

"Shove over," I say.

He shakes his head. "It's my truck."

"It's not much of a truck anymore."

"You're an idiot, Liam." But he shifts his legs so I can move in beside him. Now my ass is out of the water, anyway. I rummage in a duffel bag and pull out a sandwich. It's slightly mashed but it's food—my school lunch from hours ago. I take a big bite and then offer him the sandwich. He waves it away. He says, "Tomorrow at this time, we'll be in a Whistler hot tub with a couple of Aussie babes of questionable virtue."

"I'll be happy when I'm back in Tremblay with Jordan."

Tej yawns. "She's probably not wasting any time thinking about you."

I ignore the barb in his voice. I poke him in the side and say, "A little jealous?"

He snorts. "Not of her. Not of anything in Tremblay."

He drains the Coke, belches, draws his sleeping bag around him and lies down. He fits this space better than I do—I have to keep my knees bent. The bed of the pickup is uncomfortably close to my face and makes me feel like I'm in a coffin.

I say, "Chances of us getting to Whistler are about as good as you ever meeting any babes."

"How long have we been friends, Liam?" He doesn't wait for me to answer. He says, "Since first grade. Now we're in twelfth grade, so that's what?" He pauses and pretends to count on his fingers. "Twelve years? In all those years, when have I ever been wrong?"

Tej doesn't know the meaning of wrong, which isn't the same as never being wrong. I say, "You don't know anything about hiking through the mountains."

"It's not exactly Everest, Einstein. And I've done some hiking."

"You've hiked. Yeah, right." Tej spends every waking hour at school or studying. He got early acceptance at three big universities.

He says I should go with him, get a job, share a place. "People disappear in the mountains, Tej."

"You want to sit here and wait for someone to find us? They'll find our sorry skeletons. No way. We'll walk out."

I finish the sandwich and wish I had another one. Could be Tej is right. Could be that tomorrow at this time we'll be sitting in McDonald,s with a tray of burgers AND the Aussie babes.

The light is gone and it's so dark I can't see Tej. I can't see my hand in front of my face. It's so dark we could be in a coffin. Panic creeps into my throat and I take a deep breath.

Tej's voice is quiet, calm. "We'll be fine, Liam." I feel his hand on my shoulder, a touch so quick it could be accidental, and then it's gone. "Trust me. I know what I'm doing."

Chapter Three

"It's barely drizzling now." Tej, ahead of me, peers up at the sky from under the hood of his jacket.

Dense cloud drapes the alpine meadow. The mountaintops are invisible. Everything looks gray.

Tej says, "We're making good time. We should be out to the highway by late afternoon."

Late afternoon. I shift my backpack to a different sore place on my shoulder. My feet are soaked and my shoes gnaw the back of my heels. "I'm starving."

Tej rolls his eyes. "We ate breakfast."

"Two granola bars are not breakfast." Actually, I'm more thirsty than hungry. I stick my tongue out to collect drops of rain. "And that was hours ago."

We're following a trail made by about a zillion elk as they traversed the alpine meadow from the valley where they wintered. The soft earth of the meadow is dug deep with their tracks. Far across the valley, the north-facing mountain slope is still covered in snow.

Water from the melting snowpack trickles in small channels and I stoop to collect some in my cupped hands. It's cold, almost ice, and it burns the back of my throat. My hands feel raw and I jam them back into my gloves. Rounded hummocks of new grass line these channels and I pick a stalk to chew. At least we have good gear. We packed for spring snowboarding conditions high on the glacier, so we have rainproof jackets, pants and gloves. We have food—power bars and dried fruit. We had sleeping bags in the truck. Tej likes to think that we'll end up in some babe's cushy condo, but it hasn't happened yet—we always end up sleeping in the truck. But we didn't bring the sleeping bags. We left almost everything behind with the truck so we could walk fast. Now I wish I'd packed a few of Tej's Cokes.

I don't know how far we've walked. Tej is in the lead, as usual. I follow the bobbing hood of his blue jacket as he picks the trail. He's a good foot shorter than me, always has been, and there's nothing to him. But he's strong. Tej and his family moved to our town partway through first grade. The teacher put him in the desk in front of me. Back then no one was moving into our town; they were all moving out. We hadn't seen a new kid in town, ever. And Tej was small, smaller than the kindergarten kids. The other boys and I probably laughed at him. Anyway, he pissed himself. No one else noticed. I did, because the puddle was right in front of my feet. I didn't say anything. At recess he showed up on the soccer field wearing his gym shorts. He walked into our soccer game like he owned it. He was fast, but more than that, he knew what to do with the ball. Tej is like that with all sports. He makes up for his small size.

Tej calls back to me, "There's a carcass up ahead. It looks like your dinner plate on rib night."

Tej and I have been friends for a long time. That makes up for his big mouth. Mostly.

Just off the path, a flock of crows haggle over the bony remains of what looks like an elk calf. Tej pauses, and I take the chance to rest. I sink down to the ground to watch the birds. Whatever got the elk didn't leave much behind. Elk bones shine white among the black of the crows. A patch of brown elk hide flaps like a small flag.

Tej tosses me a power bar. I say, "Just one?"

"We have a ways to go. We don't want

to eat everything at once." He sits down on the ground beside me.

"I do."

One crow is using its big black beak to saw into the spine bones of the calf. Another snags the bit of hide and flies off with it.

I tear into the power bar. The bar is hard to chew and I wish I had a bottle of water. Tej is eating his bar in small bits. I finish mine and watch him eat his.

"A bear has been through here," he says.

I follow his gaze just off the trail to a pile of black scat. "Nice." I wrinkle my nose. The poo is pebbled with red. "What's it been eating?"

Tej leans closer to the pile. I think about pushing him into it, but of course I don't. He says, "Looks like bear berries from last fall. Berries that stay on the bush over the winter are sweet."

"Bear berries?"

"Kinnikinnick is the real word. Bears love them."

That's the other thing about Tej. He actually pays attention in biology.

"Any shoelaces in that scat?"

"Bears don't eat people." He toes the grass around the pile. "Good thing too, because this bear can't be too far away." He points to the fresh green grass under the scat. "What bears really like to eat is dead things." He points to the elk. "Like that."

We've seen bears when we were fishing and along the highway. My dad says that when he was a kid, bears used to come into town in the spring. You can't be afraid of bears or you'd never leave the house. You just have to give them enough room. I glance around me.

Tej elbows me. "You want the rest of this?" He hands me his half-eaten power bar.

I grab it and cram it into my mouth.

Tej shakes his head. "You're as bad as those crows. Come on, let's get moving."

No complaint from me, not if there is a bear anywhere close. I take a last look at the elk bones and start walking again.

The trail drops down into a grove of aspen. The leaves on the trees are so new that the branches seem to glow green. Here the trail breaks into strands between the trees. In some places I have to turn sideways to fit between the tree trunks. Despite the drizzle, I'm starting to sweat. The ground is roped with tree roots and everything is slimy with rain. The white bark of the trees is gashed by the elk that eat the bark in the winter. I'm so hungry I think about the bark. But it's water I want. The power bar is like a brick in my belly and it's sucking up all my moisture. When I see a rivulet of meltwater, I kneel down and take off my gloves. As I scoop my hands into the tiny stream, I notice a flattened smear of mud along the water. The back of my throat sticks together.

"Tej!" It comes out as a croak. I try again. "Tej!"

He stops and turns back. I point to the track in the mud. "Bear."

Tej stoops to examine the track. He whistles.

The track is twice the size of my glove, a

fat five-toed pad marked with curved claws. Big claws. I know from the size of the track, but the claws confirm it. Black bear tracks don't show much claw.

"That's a good-sized grizzly."

I can't trust my voice, so I nod.

Tej straightens up and says, "If we're going to make it before nightfall, we better pick up the pace."

"Nightfall?" I scramble to my feet and follow him.

He speaks without turning his head. "I thought we'd be out by now. The trail must not follow a straight line."

He plows through the undergrowth and branches snap in my face. I say, "Like the elk herd made a nice straight path for us to follow?"

"Fairly straight. Or at least I thought so. With the cloud cover, I can't tell our direction so well."

"But you know where we are."

"Of course. I think we should climb back out above the trees. Maybe we're too low."

I won't mind being in the open. We find

a path that is wide enough that our packs don't snag on the branches and make our way up. By the time we break free of the trees, my thighs are burning and we're both panting. Under my pack, sweat plasters my jacket to my back. The clouds hang even lower and the drizzle hardens to rain. Below us, the trees are shrouded in mist. It's like the rain is erasing where we've been. Tej pauses.

"Maybe we should go back down, try to get into the valley."

My jaw drops. "We were hours hiking up!"

He scans the horizon. For a second, he looks worried, but when he turns to me, any concern is gone from his face. "You have a better idea, brainiac?"

I spin on my heel and head back the way we've just come, leaving Tej behind me. In Tej's smaller tracks, I purposely stomp. It's not his fault that we're here. It's not his fault we took the forestry road, even though everyone knows it's too early to be on the back roads. They're labeled "summer only" on the maps for a reason, Tej. It's not his fault that the truck rolled, even though he oversteers. It's not his fault that it's raining, although if the sun were shining, he'd take credit for that. I could have studied the map, tried to figure out a route to the highway. But Tej is better at that than I am. He's smarter at everything. He's the one who's leaving Tremblay after graduation and happy to be going. He's the one who wants me to go too, get a real job, a city job. Tej is the one who sets the plays and makes the decisions. I can hear Tej behind me, and I know he's half-running to match my pace.

In the fringe of aspen, I stop dead. Tej stumbles into my back. "What?"

On the trail ahead of me, among our own clear footprints, I see the tracks of a grizzly bear. The paw prints flatten ours. The impressions from the bear's clawed toes cover the toes of our boot prints. It's like the bear was trying to remove our marks from the trail.

"It's following us." I look over both my shoulders. "The bear is stalking us."

Chapter Four

"It was going the same direction. That doesn't mean it's following us." Tej glances around him, and then he shouts, "Okay, bear, the meadow is all yours. We're going down to the valley."

I slam my hand over Tej's mouth. "You're telling it where we are. It's like ringing a dinner bell."

Tej knocks my hand away. "You don't think the bear knows exactly where we are?" He sniffs at his underarms and then mine. "He knows."

I peer into the deepening forest. "It must be close."

Tej nods. "It's just waiting for us to get out of his way." He steps in front of me on the path. "So let's get out of his way."

I'm not too proud to say I'm glad Tej is going first. But every hair on my back prickles when I think the bear might go for the straggler at the rear. I match my pace to Tej's, sticking to him so close I can hear him breathing. He says, "We've probably walked this close to bears a hundred times. They don't want to cross paths with us any more than we want to meet up with them. You just don't want to surprise one."

Suddenly I wish I carried one of those lame little bells the tourists use to make noise in the woods.

I can hear rain pattering on the leaves overhead, but the canopy of branches acts like an umbrella. The trees are dense and sometimes I have to stoop to get under the branches. It's darker in the forest. I stumble over a tree root and crash into Tej. He swears, and then he says, "Watch your big feet."

It's stupid but I feel like crying. My muscles are on fire; my empty stomach has stopped rumbling and now aches.

On cue, the rain turns to a torrent and crashes through the canopy of aspen to pour down on us. We tighten our hoods, but it feels like rain is running down my back. Tej is shivering. He says, "We should think about making a camp."

"You mean spend the night out here?"

"It's getting too dark to hike. You don't want to fall in the dark and risk breaking something." He steps off the path and scans the forest.

"But you said…"

He lifts his hand to stop me. "If you want to keep walking, go right ahead."

He knows I won't, and I hate him a little for being so sure of that. "You have a lighter to make a fire?"

He nods. "Matches."

I sigh. "I'll find some wood."

This makes us both laugh. We're in the middle of a forest, after all.

We set up camp in the lee of an overturned pine tree, its shallow roots still encased in a plate of dirt. The roots form a back wall for our shelter and a bit of overhang for a roof. Not much overhang—we won't both fit in the sliver of dry ground.

"Look for some small deadfall. We can make a lean-to." Tej takes off his pack and settles himself under the overhang out of the rain.

"We?" I sling my pack next to him.

You'd think that in a forest it would be easy to collect small tree trunks and branches. Not. Fallen trees are heavy, and small ones in the ground are too green to snap. I haul what I can back to the shelter. I'm sweating and want more than anything to take off my jacket. But the rain would douse me in seconds. I set the bigger trunks up against the dirt overhang, and then I layer on branches to form a barrier from the rain. I set small green branches on the floor of the shelter as a mattress between the wet ground and our butts. It is small, but the shelter keeps the worst of the rain off.

Tej has gathered a pile of twigs and small branches. He's shredding bark with his knife. He says, "We need more dry wood for the fire."

I look at the heap I've already hauled to the shelter. "More?"

"Do you have to question everything I say?" He reaches for another piece of bark and attacks it with his knife.

"You're going to cut yourself."

He tells me to commit a physically impossible sex act.

I say, "I'll make the fire. You get more wood."

His look says what he doesn't have to: *You can't make a fire.*

I say, "One match. I do it all the time."

"To light a bush fire with half a can of white gas." But he stands up and tosses me the matches. Then he plods off to get firewood.

I choose a spot for the fire in the opening of the shelter, not so close that we burn ourselves down, but under the overhang of the tree roots to keep as much rain out of the fire as possible. I arrange bark strips, shredding some even finer with my fingers. I take out a match, wooden, waterproof—trust Tej to think of packing these—and scrape the match head against the package. It flares, and I set the flame to the pile of bark. It catches. A strand of smoke lifts from the tiny pile. I grab some twigs to feed the fire, and in that instant the fire sputters out.

This time I pull everything I need close at hand. I add more bark strips to the pile and light it. The flame is bright and I feed it a small twig. Then another. The twigs are damp, everything is, and the fire fades to a red ember. I drop to my knees and blow gently. The fire catches again and I hold a twig in the flame, puffing air into the flame. I grab another twig, and another. Smoke is burning my eyes, but I keep blowing on the fire. I have to get it burning hot enough to add bigger bits of wood. I'm kneeling over the fire, my butt in the air, feeling like I've finally got the fire started, when I hear a branch snap in the forest right next to the shelter.

I sit upright. New sweat prickles under my arms. "Tej?"

No answer.

I peer into the trees. My mouth is suddenly so dry that my tongue feels like a sock. "That wasn't funny, Tej."

Nothing. I yank back my hood so I can hear better. Rain sizzles into my small fire. "Okay, Mr. Bear. You can piss off now."

The forest is quiet.

I want fire and I want it now. I look down at my fire to find it's gone out. With shaking hands I grab more bark, lots of it, and put a match to it. And another match, just for good measure. I toss on a twig, blowing hard so that the flame jumps, and then add a bigger twig. The fire is going, but my head is light from blowing on it.

More twigs. I dump on a handful. Smoke pours from the fire and I empty my lungs into it, but the twigs drop into the fire, smothering it. Again, the fire dies.

Nothing I'm saying is polite enough to repeat.

I grab the last of the shredded bark. "Light. Please light." I set the match to the bark, holding it until it burns down to my fingers. Puff. Puff. Twigs, one at a time. Don't look away from the fire. Puff. It's starting to crackle. A bigger twig. More smoke, but the fire is strong. Grab a small branch. Breathe on the fire. The fire is the size of a basketball now. I snap dry branches over my shin and feed these to the blaze.

"You got it going."

Tej's voice makes me jump. He's returned to the shelter with his arms full of dead branches. He drops these into the pile, and then he stoops next to the fire. Taking a branch from me, he stacks it on the fire. Then he holds his hand out. "Matches."

I hand him the package. He shakes it and gives me a look.

We pile up wood at the entrance to the shelter and crawl in. I add more wood to the fire. The fire is like a furnace. More than that, it's like a barricade.

I tell Tej about hearing the noise in the forest.

He says, "Liam, if that bear had wanted us, he'd be eating us now."

I look out through the smoke into the woods. It's dark now, too dark to see. I put another stick on the fire. I feed that fire all night long, only falling asleep with the first light of dawn.

Chapter Five

During the night the sky clears, which is good because the rain has stopped. But without the cloud cover, it's cold. Our breath puffs out like smoke. Every joint in my body is complaining. Hunger wrings my guts.

Tej isn't wasting any time. He's got his woolen snowboarding toque pulled down low over his ears and he's walking fast.

"I think I know where we went wrong yesterday."

I can hear the shiver in his voice.

He continues, "When we went off the road, we must have been farther north than we thought. That's why we didn't reach the highway. But we can't be far now."

I stride along behind him. We're keeping to a well-worn deer trail. Tej says it's the right direction, more or less. The dense undergrowth among the trees makes a more direct route impossible. In an opening, I call for Tej to stop. "Just for a minute."

Nature's call. I leave the path for a bit of privacy, just far enough that I'm out of sight of Tej. As I'm doing up my pants, I spot a quick movement on the forest floor. A bird bursts into flight right under my nose, which makes me jump. Just inches from my right foot is a small nest of eggs.

I kneel down to inspect the nest. The eggs are the size of the end of my thumb, five of them, pale brown with speckles. They blend so well with the ground that if the bird hadn't flown up, I never would have seen the nest. Probably I was just about to step on it. I would have crushed the eggs and the adult bird.

My stomach rumbles. Eggs. Protein.

Not that I'm a fan of raw eggs. I like my eggs fried so the yolk is solid but still soft.

My stomach gurgles and growls.

These eggs are so small I bet I could swallow them whole. I pick up an egg. It feels warm in my palm. The forest falls quiet all of a sudden, as if it knows I'm taking an egg. I look around for the adult bird but nothing is moving. I'll just take two, one for me and one for Tej. I select another egg.

Tej is saying something, but I can't hear what it is. His voice sounds high-pitched, like a whine.

It's stupid, but finding these eggs makes me feel powerful, like we could make it out here, if we had to. I straighten up and take a couple of steps toward the path.

Tej is standing with his back to me, his arms straight at his sides. I can see his shoulders moving as he breathes, the exhaled air puffing out as if he's panting. Then he sucks in his breath.

Just on the other side of Tej, something big and brown is on the trail. It shifts and now I know why Tej is scared witless. It's a bear.

Chapter Six

I try to call to Tej but my voice barely squeaks. The bear is on all fours, swaying its head back and forth, sniffing the air. Its brown fur is tipped with lighter brown, and its eyes, close to the middle of its face, are round and black. Its ears are like brown tennis balls on the side of its head. The bear is looking at Tej, and then it sees me. I feel the eggs slip out of my hand.

We are so close to the bear I can smell it, a gagging smell that is rank and sweet at the same time. The bear rears up, getting a better look at us.

Tej backs into me. He speaks to me in a singsong voice, trying to soothe the bear, I guess. "Walk backward, you idiot." I force my feet to shuffle backward on the path. "Slowly," he says. "Don't make eye contact with it. And don't run or he'll charge for sure."

Tej is between the bear and me. I could turn and run right now, and the bear would get him. I'd get away and the bear would get Tej. I think about this for a shamefully long time, but then I do as Tej says.

The bear on its hind legs is as tall as Tej, maybe as tall as me. So long as the bear is on its hind legs, we're all right. A bear can't charge on two legs.

The bear drops to all fours.

Tej mutters, "Crap."

Good thing I already did.

The bear lowers its head. When a dog looks like this, it means you could get bitten. When a bear looks like this, it means you could be lunch. The bear's eyes harden, as if it has lost patience with us. We're on his trail and he wants us off. The bear opens its jaws. Big jaws. Really big teeth. His jaws make a smacking sound.

I whisper, "He's going to eat us."

Tej is backing up faster now. He says, "For once in your life, you might be right."

I reach down for a rock.

The bear huffs, and then it sweeps its front paw across the path. Big paw. Really big claws. Dirt sprays up. I feel a clod of mud hit my cheek.

The rock in my hand is the size of a cantaloupe. I don't know why I'm holding it—a rock is useless against a bear.

The bear huffs and pops its jaw.

A bad sign, a very bad sign.

The bear shakes its head like it's making up its mind. Then it charges.

Tej goes totally still. The bear is so close now I can see bits of dried grass in its fur. Saliva hangs in ropes from its jaws. Its eyes are flat black. It's not so much a decision as a reaction—I lob the rock up.

The toss is so weak I could be pitching to first-grade T-ballers. But it arcs straight up over Tej, hangs in the air and then plummets. The rock clunks square in the center of the bear's skull.

The bear blinks and rears back onto its ass. It shakes its head and lets out a bawling wail. Then it runs away from us, up the trail in the direction we came.

Tej bursts out laughing. "It was just a yearling," Tej says. "Hardly more than a cub."

I'm not laughing, not yet. My knees are jelly and my hands are shaking. "Right, just a teddy bear."

On the ground by my feet is a mess of smashed egg. I lean down. Two miniature birds lie folded in the broken yellow sacs.

Chapter Seven

"If that bear was just a yearling, I'd hate to see it when it's full-grown."

We're in an open meadow of long grass. Ahead of me on the trail, Tej waves his hand. "I'd hate to see it with its mother. We'd be hamburger."

"You would be. I'd still be running."

"You can't outrun a bear, Liam. They're faster than they look. Remember that video my dad took of the grizzly getting the sheep?"

I remember. It was at his uncle's ranch in Montana. Tej's dad had videotaped the grizzly from his truck. The bear was in Tej's uncle's sheep pasture, chasing the flock. The video showed the bear taking the sheep, lunging with its front paws to bring the sheep down, and then tearing into the sheep with its teeth. It didn't take long for that sheep to die. I say, "Your uncle shot the bear, and then he yelled at your dad for sitting there with his camera instead of doing something to save his sheep."

Tej says, "That's right. You think you could have run faster than that bear?"

I think about how fast that yearling bear closed the distance between it and us, how it drove with its front legs, how its shoulders rolled with each long stride.

I say, "The bear got the slowest sheep. I don't have to outrun the bear. It's like Darwin said about survival of the fastest. I just have to be faster than you."

"Ha ha. Darwin's theory is survival of the fittest, by the way, and mental fitness counts. Human beings didn't get to the top of the food chain by being big and dumb."

I wish that sounded more like a joke. "By big and dumb, you're talking about the bear, right?"

He either ignores me or doesn't hear me. Probably he's ignoring me. Tej pauses on the trail. "Look," he says, "you can see where a bear has been eating."

The meadow grass has been cropped into jagged swaths. "Bears eat grass?"

Tej nods. "In the spring they do, when the grass is high in protein."

I pull a stalk of grass and chew it. It tastes like, well, grass. "Just grass?"

"Pretty much, until the berries ripen." Tej starts walking. "They'll hunt if it's easy, like a young or wounded elk."

"Or a nice fat sheep in a pasture."

"That was unusual, apparently."

"Maybe the bear took the elk calf we saw yesterday."

"If it didn't, it probably ate it anyway. Anything dead is food for a bear."

I look over my shoulder for the hundredth

time, just in case that yearling brings its mama to kick some human butt. Nice fresh human butt. I step up closer to Tej. "I sure nailed it with that rock."

Tej laughs. "I've heard of bears running away with bullets in their skull. I don't think your rock did much damage."

I say, "Well, I guess I scared it away, which is more than you did."

"The bear was just bluffing. It wouldn't have attacked us."

"Oh, and you weren't scared at all."

He turns to look at me. "You're scared of bears because you don't understand them. Like you don't understand most things."

I know where this is going. "If this is about me leaving Tremblay with you, I understand enough."

He shakes his head. "You don't. You only understand what you know, and all you know is Tremblay. It's a big, wide world out there, Liam." He sneers. "The only thing big and wide in Tremblay is Jordan Campbell's ass." He laughs.

I feel my face go red. "Is that supposed to be a joke, Tej?"

He shakes his head. "Of course it's a joke. You have no sense of humor." He sniggers. "Maybe Jordan has sucked it out of you."

"Maybe you should shut up about Jordan."

"She's holding you back, my friend."

I move in close to his face. "I'd rather be in Tremblay with Jordan than go live in some crap-hole college apartment with a bunch of guys who smoke and talk about girls because they never get a girl and never will because they're so friggin' conceited."

Tej looks a bit like the bear right now. His eyes have the same maniac gleam. He says, "There's nothing wrong with being an intellectual."

"There is if you're also an asshole."

He flips me the bird. "Fine. Rot in Tremblay. Work in the mill for as long as it stays open. Or pump gas. Any idiot can pump gas. Marry Jordan and have six kids.

She'll already have a couple of her own from bedding everyone else in town, but what's a few more?"

My face is burning, and I feel my hands forming fists. "Jordan likes me the way I am. She doesn't try to make me into something else. And just because she turned you down for a date doesn't make her a whore. If it did, then every girl in Tremblay would be a whore."

For a second it looks like he's going to take a swing at me, but then he drops his arm. He tips his head. "Do you hear that?"

"What?"

He holds up his hand. "Listen." He cocks his head. "It's a siren. An ambulance or something."

I can hear it now, but barely. "On the highway."

Tej breaks into a grin. "The highway."

We start to run.

Chapter Eight

I'm in the lead now, running in the direction of the sound of the highway. Tej is panting to keep up, but I don't care if I'm leaving him in my dust. I'm thinking about hamburgers, a six-patty monster dripping with cheese. And milkshakes. Chocolate. Strawberry. Both. And apples, a whole bag of apples. And pizza. My legs burn and the back of my throat feels like I've swallowed a scrub brush. "Hurry!"

We're charging up a slope strewn with rocks. Behind me, Tej stumbles and I turn to haul him to his feet. The sound of the siren has faded to nothing, but it plays in my memory. The highway. We're going home!

The slope grows steep and I have to scramble. I use my hands to pull myself up the rocks. Finally, the slope flattens to a broad plateau.

Tej calls from below me. "Can you see it?"

The light is getting flat. "It must be over the rise." I wait for Tej to catch up, and then I start running again.

I don't know what makes me stop, but I do, and good thing. At the edge of the rise, the ground falls away down a sheer rock face, so far down that it makes me dizzy. I fall to my knees.

Tej runs up behind me and I yank him by his legs to stop him from going over the precipice. He takes a look over the edge. "Oh no."

We can see the highway, all right. It

snakes through the valley far below us. Cars on the highway look the size of toys. Tej flips on his cell phone and then swears as he snaps it closed again. "Nothing." He jumps to his feet and starts shouting at the cars, "Hey, we're here!"

"We're too far away. They'll never see us."

Still shouting, he waves his hands over his head.

"Like that's going to make a difference."

He throws himself on the ground beside me. "Well, I found the highway. Now we just have to get down to it."

I scan the rock face. "We'll kill ourselves if we try to climb." I'm so hungry I'm half-tempted to try it.

He says, "We'll climb down the backside of the mountain and circle around to the highway."

Up here, we're at the edge of everything we know. The highway leads home. One of those cars could be my dad. I swallow a lump in my throat. "I can't do it, Tej."

Clouds roll around us, deadening the last light of the afternoon. I watch the highway vanish in the cloud. Maybe it was there all day yesterday and we just couldn't see it. I shiver, suddenly cold.

"We can do it, Liam."

"We'll be out here another night."

Tej nods. "Maybe. We'll walk as long as we can."

With a resigned sigh, I hoist myself to my feet.

Tej takes a granola bar out of his pocket. "The last one." He rips the package and hands me half. The bar is basically crumbs. I put it in my mouth, not even tasting it. It's our last bite of food, night is dropping on us, and somewhere out there a bear could be just as hungry as we are.

Chapter Nine

Down. Down. Just keep walking down. One foot. The other foot. Down. Down. Down.

It's fully dark now, so dark that I have to keep my nose at Tej's pack to be able to see him. The ground is uneven and my knees are sore from jamming my feet in holes. We don't stop to rest because when we stop, our sweat starts to freeze. So we walk. Down. Down.

We break back into the trees about midnight. The clouds thickened through the evening so that the stars and moon have disappeared. There is nothing but black sky. In the trees, I stop trying to see. Tej walks with his hands in front of his face to sweep away the tree branches, and I follow in his path. If he stumbles on a root or fallen tree, I fall on top of him. We're not talking because there's nothing to say. We're walking. Down.

We're making enough noise, what with the branches we're breaking. If there's anything in this forest, it knows we're here. And it knows we're crazy.

Crazy. I feel a light touch on the back of my neck and it makes me spin. A white flash of under-wing appears as a bird swoops across the path behind me and disappears into a high tree.

"An owl!" I grab Tej by the pack and point up into the tree. "It touched me as it flew past!"

Tej shakes his head. "Too bad, Liam. That means the owl is calling you to die."

I check his face to make sure he's joking. He grins.

"Not," I say. "That's if you hear an owl call your name."

"I'd say that if an owl actually taps you on the shoulder, it really wants you."

"Well, I'm not planning on packing it in."

"I don't know, Liam. Looks like you're going to win the Darwin Award—you're dying young and stupid before you can pass along your genes. Our species is better for it."

He turns to continue walking and slams headfirst into a thick branch. "Ow!"

I laugh. "Looks like I'm in good company. We must be the Darwin Expedition."

Tej rubs his head. "The forest is too thick to walk in at night. We'll stop and get a fire going. It'll be light in a few hours and we can start again."

Images of hamburgers and milkshakes dissolve in my mind. I toss my pack on the ground. I watch while Tej gets a fire going, and in the light of the small blaze we gather deadfall. The trees are so dense right here that there's little undergrowth. But the fire could spread to the trees, so we keep it small, feeding it branches to keep it going.

We hug the fire, Tej on one side, me on the other. Across the fire, Tej's face glows red. His eyes are half-closed. He sits with his knees drawn up to his chest. "That bear that took my uncle's sheep?" Tej pauses. Then he says, "They never caught that bear."

"I thought you said your uncle shot it."

"He did. But the bear ran off. They tried to find it, and they set traps. They actually caught it too. But it broke out of the trap, left two of its toes behind."

My stomach does an unpleasant roll. "That would make for one pissed-off bear."

"They tried to trap it again, but it was on to them. Every year they set traps, but no matter how they try to disguise the trap, the bear sniffs it out." Tej's voice is slow with sleep. "They never catch it. It comes into the pasture every spring and takes a sheep. Then it buggers off. They know it's the same bear because of its three-toed tracks."

I put another branch on the fire. "Payback time for the bear?"

Tej rolls onto his side and puts his head on the ground. "I think the bear wakes up hungry from hibernating all winter. So it eats a sheep. Then it goes away and does normal bear things."

Normal bear things. If a bear eats an elk calf, or a sheep, how weird is it to think a bear might eat a human? Or maybe Tej is right—bears don't eat humans. But they might give us a swat that crushes our skull. A bear could crack our heads just like I broke those eggs when I dropped them.

"Last year my uncle saw smaller tracks too, like the bear had brought a cub. My uncle thinks the bear was teaching the cub to avoid traps. And about the taste of mutton." Tej closes his eyes.

I listen to Tej's breathing deepen as he sleeps. I don't feel sleepy. I'm beyond tired. I lean back against a tree. The fire feels good. I let the heat of the flames soak into my feet and shins. I hold my hands out, warming them over the fire. I feed the fire and listen to it crackle and pop. My eyes get heavy.

The bear's jaws made that same popping sound.

I jerk my head up. That was hours ago and miles away. The bear is long gone.

I wonder if the owl has found some tasty rodent to eat. Yum. I let my head drop back against the tree.

It's all about food, really, for owls and bears. My stomach rumbles. And for me. Food and sex. I don't have personal experience with the sex part. Tej thinks that's all Jordan and I do. Not. Jordan isn't in a hurry to have sex. And I don't mind too much. I like that Jordan is happy with me.

Tej sets the bar high for people. Jordan could be royalty and she wouldn't be good enough, not in Tej's opinion. He's like that with everyone. He's really hard on himself.

I don't know how he puts up with me.

I fall asleep, I'm sure, because when I wake up, the fire is out and Tej is sitting up straight, peering into the trees. The first strands of dawn lighten the forest. Tej's hat is covered in a light dusting of snow.

"What?" I try to follow his stare. A skiff of new snow coats the ground.

Tej scrambles to his feet. "It was nothing, just a branch snapping. A squirrel probably."

I heave myself up. Every muscle in my body complains. My clothes feel damp and chilled. I shiver. I turn to take a leak. Tej swings his pack on. "Come on," he says. "We need to move."

"Yeah, yeah." I watch the snow steam yellow.

"Now, Liam."

I look at Tej's face. He's shivering and pale. His lips are blue. "Okay." I zip up. That's when I see them, clearly marked in the fresh snow, a stone's throw from where we slept—the big-clawed tracks of a grizzly.

Chapter Ten

"Is it the same bear?"

Tej's teeth chatter when he speaks. "More than one bear," he says.

"More than one?" Tracks lace in and out of the trees around our camp. In one place I can see where a bear plunked its butt on the ground. It's a large impression in the snow. Very large.

Tej points to a set of tracks off to the side. "Those are bigger tracks."

Almost twice the size. I swallow.

Tej says, "Could be a sow and the yearling, or a different yearling and its mother. But it's more than one bear, for sure."

Despite the cold, I'm sweating.

He motions with his hand. "Come on."

I don't question Tej on that. We take off through the trees. Snow from the branches plops on our heads; the ground is slippery. Tej falls and I pull him up by his pack. "Let me go first."

He doesn't speak, just steps in behind me. That should have been my first clue. When Tej is silent, something is wrong. I glance behind me to find he's dropped way back. "Pick up the pace, Tej!"

He stands and looks at me.

"What the...?" I walk back to him.

He drops down to his knees. "I'm tired. I need to rest."

I yank on his arm. "We just started. Get up."

"I'm cold."

"So am I. If you walk faster, you'll warm up."

"Maybe you should just go."

I yank on his arm, hard enough that he should cry out. But he doesn't. "Tej, you're talking like a crazy person. I'm not going to leave you."

"I don't know where we are, Liam. I never knew. I just said I did. When I heard that siren yesterday, I thought we were out, but we're not. And I don't know how to get out. We're going to die and they'll never even find our bones."

"You don't know where we are?" Whatever concern I felt for him vanishes. "You never knew?" I reach down with both hands and haul him to his feet. "Well, thank you for bringing me with you." I shove him in the chest. "For taking the stupid forestry road in the first place. For rolling your truck and almost killing us right then and there." I shove him again. "For hanging off my ass since first grade."

"I didn't force you to take this trip."

"No, you just expected I would. Like you expect me to do everything you want. You know how often I've turned down parties because they didn't invite you too? You know how often I've gone to parties with people you like, and I sit there all night wishing I were anywhere else?"

Tej looks away from me.

"I'm sick of you. I'm sick of the way you talk to me. I'm sick of your so-called jokes about Jordan." I suck in a breath. "Don't you ever say anything about Jordan again. I never should have listened to you about anything. I'll be happy when you leave town, Tej. Then I can get on with my own life."

His voice is small. "So, go. Piss off."

"I will." I take a step away from him.

"When I leave Tremblay, I'm not coming back."

"Good. We'll be a better town for it."

"You don't know where you're going either, Einstein."

"Like I care. At least I'll be rid of you."

I break into a run. Tree branches snag on my pack. I rip off my pack and leave it. The downward grade increases and I bounce against the trees, pinballing down the mountain. I don't think I could stop even if I wanted to. My head starts to spin and I grab onto a tree to slow myself.

Maybe all that has kept those bears from killing us is that we're two people together. Maybe, apart, they'll pick us off. Or maybe they'll be satisfied with Tej.

Tej. I look back the way I've come. I can't see him.

He doesn't mean to be a butthead, I know that. I know him. When we snowboard together, or play sports, or watch movies, he's the best guy on the planet. He just can't stand being wrong. He gets a hundred percent on a math test, and then he agonizes over the bonus question he missed. And with me, he'll bluff rather than admit he made a mistake.

He's scared about leaving Tremblay, I know he is. I'm scared about him leaving. He's still leading, but I'm not following, not this time. I don't quite know where that leaves me.

In football, I love the long bombs that

bring the crowd to its feet. But sometimes the best play is into the thickest resistance. These plays aren't spectacular, but they are solid and what you expect, a few yards gained each time. That's the way it is with Tej: not always what you want, but solid and predictable. I head back up the mountain.

I find Tej about halfway up, picking his way from tree to tree. He doesn't look surprised. I guess I'm predictable too. He doesn't say anything to me, just takes the lead again. And I let him.

The sky has lightened so that blue shows now and then. Otherwise we'd never have seen the far-off plume of smoke. Not a forest fire, not when it's been so wet. Man-made smoke. Like from a smokestack.

Chapter Eleven

Tej surveys the rock face above us. "Looks like granite. The smoke could be coming from a quarry," he says. We're perched at the edge of a scree slope that extends above us and then down a good ways through a gully to a creek. We can't see any buildings; they must be too far away.

The scree is basically flat shards of rock smaller than my hand, but the slope is dotted with a few chunks the size of soccer balls. I heft one of the bigger rocks and lob it down the slope. It rolls a couple of times and then catches air, bouncing down the slope. Behind, it leaves a light-colored wake of the smaller rock.

Tej whistles. "It's like liquid rock."

"Or snow. We can boot-ski."

Tej looks at me. "It'll shred you if you fall."

"I don't plan on falling."

"That's because you're an idiot." He peers down the gully. "It's a friggin' double black diamond."

"Sounds like you're scared." I make a chicken sound.

"Smart and scared are not the same thing. I just happen to know the logical consequence of doing something stupid."

I ignore the superior tone in his voice. "You even smell like a chicken." I sniff the air. "Like you've pissed yourself. Again."

"I don't smell anything." Tej sniffs too. "Oh wait, I do. It smells like you, only more."

A rock slithers past us on the scree slope.

I say, "You smell like a tipped port-a-potty."

"Only you would tip a port-a-potty."

"You've tipped port-a-potties. I've seen you do it."

He says, "Okay, only you would tip a port-a-potty, then smell it."

Another rock dances past us on a crazy descent. Tej and I look up at the same time.

At the same time we say, "Uh-oh."

The bear. Same big brown face, same black eyes. I had a good look at it yesterday, and I know it's the same bear. It's above us, one big paw paused on the rocks, as if it was going to cross the gully and then it saw us. It is ten feet away. I want to swallow, but I have no spit.

The bear looks down as if it's embarrassed we spotted it. A load of bear poo plops out its rear.

"Stay still," Tej hisses. "It wants to get to the grass at the other side of the gully."

I glance across. Along the scree trail, grass grows in a tall swath.

More rock skitters down from the bear's paw.

I say, "If that thing steps onto the scree, it'll slide down and end up in our laps."

Tej shakes his head. "It'll clear the gully in one stride."

"So why isn't it?"

Just then, the grass on the other side of the gully starts to thrash. A massive brown hump appears above the grass. Then a set of ears. Big ears. Really big ears. Mama bear ears.

She's the mother bear, and we're between her and her cub.

"Damn."

The big bear rolls her head and looks right at us. Her head is as wide across as my chest and as big as a medicine ball. Her big black nose works the air, her nostrils flaring as she tries to catch our scent. She was chewing on something, grass maybe, but she's stopped chewing as she looks at us.

"Tej, we have to move."

Tej's jaw hangs open.

The female bear drops her head. Her jowls puff out and she huffs, a sound that's so deep in her chest it's more like a growl. The yearling bawls.

I'm on my feet in a low crouch, but Tej seems frozen in his boots.

The mother bear thrusts her head through the grass and pops her jaw, wide. Suddenly we have a view of all her teeth. She lets out a rumble that sounds like a truck.

I grab Tej by his pack and hoist him to his feet. "Go!" I point him downhill and shove him onto the slope.

The sow bear takes a leap toward me that makes the ground shudder. The yearling hightails it up the scree slope, its back legs windmilling in the rock for traction. The young bear slips back a bit and then digs hard to make its way up the slope. Rocks fly off its back paws and careen down the slope. One zings past my left ear and I duck.

The mother bear lunges again. For an instant, I think about the sheep Tej's dad videotaped. I wonder if the sheep knew the bear was going to get it. I wonder if the sheep felt anything just before the bear sunk its claws into it and yanked it to its death.

Without even looking, I jump out into the scree.

Chapter Twelve

My right foot lands and immediately I start sailing down the slope. It's is steeper than anything I've boarded on. I lean back to keep my balance and take another bounding leap into the loose rock.

In any other time and place, this could be fun. I glance over my shoulder to see the large butt of the mother bear disappearing above me. Below me, I can just see Tej's head. Rocks blow past me and I call out to Tej, "Rocks!"

Each time I land, I traverse for as long as I can in order to stay up and try to check my speed. I reach back with one hand, using it like a rudder. The rocks shred my gloves. The other hand I extend out for some ballast.

My heels slip out from under me and I land on my butt. I struggle to regain my footing. My boot dislodges a good-sized rock and it takes on speed, rolling in front of me and spinning into the air.

"Tej!"

He is totally in the wrong place. We should be close together so the rocks I kick up won't build such speed. I'm back on my feet, leaping almost straight down the mountain. I'm gaining on Tej. I can see the rocks bouncing past him. One catches him in the shoulder. He ducks another, and then he takes a big one in the back of the leg. He cries out. His legs buckle and he sinks onto the rocks.

"Stay up, man!"

I see him fighting to get his balance, but rocks are screaming by him and he ducks his head. His shoulder catches and as quick as I can scream his name, he's airborne.

He rotates once, slowly, and hits the rocks. I hear the air slam out of his lungs. He bounces, spinning now, his arms flailing at his sides. I see his hands scrambling on the rocks, trying to get a hold, trying to slow down.

"Tej!" I throw my arms forward with each leap, trying to make up the distance between us.

Tej is tumbling now, rolling on the rocks, ricocheting into the air, hitting the rocks again.

My feet feel hot from friction. My gloves are hanging in pieces.

Tej spills out of the gully onto a fan of scree as the slope flattens into the valley. I hit this too and it feels like sudden slow motion. Tej is sliding on his back. He's jabbing his feet into the rocks, trying to keep from rolling again.

"Hang on!" Rock dust coats my tongue and throat. My eyes are streaming from the air rushing by. I reach out and grab the collar of Tej's jacket.

Finally, we stop. I collapse beside him. "Are you okay?"

Nothing.

I pull myself onto my knees. His eyes are open, but he's not looking at me. Then his eyes roll to white.

Chapter Thirteen

I bend close to Tej's mouth. His breath rasps in my ear.

"You're alive." My throat closes on a lump. Then my empty stomach lurches and I retch a wad of green onto the rocks. His face is laced with cuts. A gash over his forehead hangs in a bloody flap. I rip off my gloves and feel the back of his neck. I've never felt a broken neck, so I don't know what I'm looking for, but I run my hand down his spine as far as I can reach.

He murmurs, and then he groans. He lifts one knee and lets it drop. His eyes focus on me. His voice croaks, "Of course I'm alive, you idiot."

I hoot and high-five him. He returns it weakly and groans. "My leg." He motions to his right foot.

His right boot is on his leg sideways. My stomach drops again and I swallow bile. I say, "You've broken it, Tej. We'll get you fixed up."

I slip a finger into the top of his boot and feel for blood. I know not to take the boot off. It seems to be about all that's holding his foot on. There's no blood, and I breathe with relief.

I have to brace his foot somehow so it doesn't move. I reach for Tej's pack and slip it off his shoulders. His wild ride ripped open the covering on the outside, but the padded interior frame is still intact. I tip the pack upside down to empty it, but there is not much left in it. Stuff must have fallen out.

"I'm going to have to straighten your foot." My stomach flip-flops.

He says, "You? No way."

"You can't do it yourself." I look at his foot. It's grotesque the way it hangs off his lower leg. "You have a better idea, Einstein?"

He eyes his mangled foot and shakes his head. No.

I set my hands on each side of his ankle. He winces. I say, "Don't be such a wuss. On the count of three."

He sighs. "One," he counts. "Two."

I close my eyes and pull.

He screams. I scream. When I open my eyes, I see the foot is more or less where it's supposed to be.

He swears and wipes tears from his face.

I slip the empty pack over his foot. The toe of his boot sticks out through the rip in the outside fabric. I fold the pack around his leg, using the internal frame as a brace. Then I crisscross the straps of the pack across his leg and pull them tight.

He holds his hand out, like he wants me to help him up.

I say, "You can't walk on that."

He gives me the "you're an idiot" look.

"Fine," I say and haul him to his feet.

He gasps, and the color drains out of his face. He grabs my shoulders to balance himself as he takes the weight off his broken ankle.

Between clenched teeth, he says, "Sit me down."

I ease him to the ground. He's panting, and sweat beads on his forehead. He swears, spits and swears again. "You'll have to carry me."

I could, but for how long? I'm not sure I'm strong enough to make it myself, never mind carrying Tej too.

I say, "I can't carry you. It will be faster if I go alone."

I look at the blood drying on his face and the pathetic job I did bracing his ankle. He's as good as dead, and anything dead is food for a bear.

As if he can read my mind, Tej says, "What if the bears come?"

I hope my voice sounds more sure than I feel. "We'll build a fire. They won't come near a fire."

He brushes away more tears. "You'll get lost."

Probably. I swallow down on my fear. "No, I won't."

He is pale and shivering. He holds his ankle and I can see the pain shooting across his face. He says, "Then the bears will get you."

I kneel down in front of him. "I have to leave you. I'll run. I'll be back before it gets dark, I promise."

He turns his head away from me. He doesn't believe me. Why should he? I look up at the sky. It's late, only a couple of hours of daylight left. And dark clouds line the horizon. What if I can't find the quarry?

What if the bears come after me?

I rummage through the spilled contents of Tej's pack.

"If you're looking for matches," he points to the scree slope, "they're probably somewhere up there under nine feet of rocks."

But I find the matches. I open the packet—there are two left.

He snorts. "Two matches? Good luck."

I say, "We can die together, right here, tonight, or I can try to get us out. But this time we have to do it my way, Tej."

He puts his head down between his knees. He looks so small sitting there. Maybe I should carry him. At least we'd be together.

He speaks without lifting his head. "Build me a fire. Then get the hell out of here."

Chapter Fourteen

Between the sound of the water gurgling in the creek and the sound of my own breath panting in my ears, I can't hear anything else. I don't want to, actually. If that sow grizzly is hunting me down, I don't want to know. I'd rather die in blissful ignorance. Under my jacket, my shirt back is wet with sweat. I'm running in the creek because the tangle of undergrowth along the sides slows me down. My pant legs are soaked to the knees. My boots are like sieves after the scree slope, and water squishes in and out as I run.

The creek climbs, and every mile feels like ten, but I've gone more than five miles, I know it. The clouds have dropped so low that if there is any smoke from the quarry, I can't see it in the cloud cover. The daylight is just about gone.

Did I leave him enough wood? If I take too long, Tej will run out of wood. If he runs out of wood, the fire will go out. If the fire goes out, he could freeze. Or the bears could come. I jam all thoughts from my head. Just run.

The rocks on the creek bed are slimy and my feet slip. It feels like I'm running with a hundred pounds hanging on each leg.

I crash through a willow tree overhanging the creek, and a flock of crows takes off from the branches. They swoop around my head, their crow voices screaming. One dive-bombs me and I feel its talon brush my shoulder. "Get away!" I swat at the birds. They take off in a clatter of cawing.

I think about the crows feeding on

the elk calf bones, their big black beaks breaking into the bones to get the marrow. I think about the crows peeling the skin back to eat the bits of fat. Then I think about them landing on Tej.

My foot slips on the rocks and I crash to my knees. A bolt of pain shoots through my kneecaps. Get up. Run. It's just a bit of pain compared to what Tej must be going through.

When we're fishing, we usually see old beer cans in the stream, and cigarette butts. But now I don't see any sign of people. I sure don't see any quarry. All I see are rocks and trees.

Maybe it wasn't smoke from a smokestack. Maybe we just imagined it. Maybe I'm running the wrong way. If Tej were here, he'd know. And if he didn't know, he'd make me feel like we'd be okay.

Fat drops of water hit my cheeks. I tell myself it is just water from the creek splashing up on my face. But it's rain. Raindrops pelt into the creek and down my neck. It's raining, and now Tej won't be able to keep the fire going.

I fall to my knees, not bothering to lift my hood against the rain. I let it pour down on me. I should never have left Tej. When the bears are done with Tej, they'll come for me. We're not going to make it. I'm too slow and too stupid and now we are going to die.

The creek water is like ice. I let it numb my hands and knees. I let it soak into my pants and up my shirt until my teeth chatter. I haul myself to the bank of the creek.

Too slow. Too stupid. I am an idiot.

Still on my hands and knees, I crawl into the trees lining the creek. In the forest, the last of the light is already gone.

Chapter Fifteen

It is black, a night so dense that trees vanish in front of my face. I walk until I collapse. I sleep, a weird half-sleep with the sound of owls in my ears. But when I wake up, the forest is black and all I hear is pounding rain. Then I walk again.

My wet clothes rub my skin raw. I'm so cold that I can't close my fingers. I've stopped shivering. It's like I have nothing left to burn. Each time I fall down and close my eyes, I think, This is it. I'm not going to wake up.

But then I do. Part of me is glad. Part of me hates that I have to get up and walk in the black forest.

I could walk with my eyes closed and it wouldn't make a difference. My face is beaten by tree branches, my eyes jabbed so often that I imagine they run with blood, not tears. Maybe I do walk with my eyes closed. Maybe that's why the lights seem to appear out of nowhere.

Lights. It takes a second for my brain to register them.

Just two lights, like headlights, not too far away. Are the lights moving? Panic blocks my chest. Don't go. Don't leave me.

I blink and rub my eyes. No. The lights are not moving.

I thrash through the forest. As I move, the lights seem to disappear, but only because of trees blocking my vision

As I get closer, I see the lights are not headlights but what looks like a gatehouse. I claw my way through the trees. I keep my hands in front of me and tear the branches out of my way.

Closer now, and I can see a lone man leaning on the gatehouse under a metal awning, smoking. He's wearing a gray uniform with a crest on the shoulder. A night watchman, maybe. I call to him, but rain is pounding on the awning—he doesn't seem to hear.

I snap branches out of my way, ripping through the undergrowth toward him. The man at the gatehouse stands straight and squints in my direction.

"Hey!" I'm out of breath and my voice is barely a rasp. "Help!"

The man drops his cigarette and reaches for something. Before I can try to shout again, he's leveled a rifle at my head.

I burst through the undergrowth into the ditch, my hands over my head. Light from the gatehouse spills onto my face. He can see me now, can't he? Again I call, "Help!"

"What the hell?" He lowers the gun.

I stumble out of the ditch and onto the road.

He looks at me, his eyes so wide I can see the whites. "You scared the crap out of me," he says. "I thought you were a bear."

Chapter Sixteen

Everything looks different from the air. The spotlight on the chopper illuminates pale egg shapes on the ground. The light slews around and makes me dizzy. The pilot speaks to me through the headset. "We're at the scree slope. But I don't see your buddy."

This is where I left him. Isn't it? It's raining so hard that the creek is spilling out of its bed. What if Tej is underwater?

I hear one medic shout, "Look at the size of that bear."

I spin to where he's looking, just upstream of the scree slope. In the spotlight, a massive grizzly bear boots it beneath the chopper. A smaller bear is hot on her heels. The bears are heading back up the stream.

The medic hoots, "She's close to a ton, I bet. Wouldn't you hate to bump into her on a dark night?" He laughs.

I remember the smell of her, the sound she made deep in her chest, the black of her gums against the yellow of her teeth.

I speak without looking away from the ground. "Maybe Tej did."

The medic falls quiet.

A glimpse of something blue makes me shout. "There!" I point to where I saw it. "Tej's jacket!"

It's raining. Why would Tej take his jacket off?

The pilot dips the nose. The trees look close enough I could touch them. "There!" I jab my finger, as if that will make the pilot see.

He nods. "It's just a jacket, son."

No. The jacket is tangled in a shrub like it's been tossed there. Or ripped off.

I try to keep my voice from cracking. "I know he's here."

The pilot and the medics exchange looks, and I know what they're thinking. If the bears really got my friend, do I want to see what's left? I say, "Put it down."

The pilot shrugs, and the medics lower the ladder.

I sense it before I see it—a movement from under a fallen tree. Tej is on his belly, crawling out. "It's him! He threw his jacket so we'd know where he was holed up."

Tej looks up at the chopper. He's coated in mud, but even from here I can see he's okay. He bursts into a grin and waves.

Chapter Seventeen

Tej loads a huge duffel bag into the back of his truck. The truck looks pretty good, now that the roof is repaired. Tej replaced the fenders and tailgate with parts from the auto wrecking yard, and he worked all summer at Dairy Queen to pay for a paint job. I pat the fender. "Nice ride."

Tej nods.

He favors his right ankle when he walks, although no one else would notice.

He was still in a cast at graduation. He got a standing ovation as he hobbled on crutches across the stage.

He closes the tailgate and says, "You can still change your mind."

I shake my head. "I got a spot on a survey crew in September. Forestry department. Might lead to something."

Tej grins. "That grizzly will be waiting for you."

The warden who helped get Tej's truck out of the bush said it wasn't likely that the bears I saw from the chopper were the ones we had seen earlier. He said bears don't stalk humans. I think the warden might be wrong, but I'm glad we didn't find out.

"If that bear finds me, I'll give her your number in Portland."

Tej looks down at the ground. "I guess Jordan isn't coming to say good-bye."

I shake my head. "No, Jordan thinks you and I need to do this by ourselves."

He laughs. "You can tell her I cried, if you want." He scuffs the ground with his shoe. "Jordan is good for you." He looks up at me. "I was wrong about her."

I smile. "Yeah, you were wrong."

Jordan got a job with the same survey crew. Jordan might lead to something too.

Tej says, "Maybe I thought if you didn't have Jordan, you'd come with me." He looks up at his house. His entire family is gathered on the front step, waiting to wave good-bye. He says, "You have everything you need here in Tremblay."

"You do too, here and in Portland. You'll be fine." I shuffle my feet. "And you never know. I might end up at tech school. I've registered for a couple of adult education classes. High-school upgrading."

He looks at me and his eyebrows shoot up.

I laugh. "You were wrong, now you're speechless? This must be a first."

"You're right, which is also a first." Tej claps me on the arm. "I'll be back at Christmas. We'll go snowboarding."

I pull him into a fast hug, and then I

give him a shove toward the door of his truck. "Yeah, and this time, I'll drive."

"Fine with me. I'll sit in the back with a couple of Aussie babes." Tej slides in behind the wheel.

"I'm beginning to think anything is possible." I close his door. "Now get the hell out of here."

Diane Tullson is the author of the ALA Best Book *Red Sea*. Diane lives in Vancouver, British Columbia.

Other titles in the
Orca Soundings series

Other titles in the
Orca Soundings series

Other titles in the
Orca Soundings series

Something Girl
Beth Goobie

Sticks and Stones
Beth Goobie

Stuffed
Eric Walters

Tell
Norah McClintock

Thunderbowl
Lesley Choyce

Tough Trails
Irene Morck

The Trouble with Liberty
Kristin Butcher

Truth
Tanya Lloyd Kyi

Wave Warrior
Lesley Choyce

Who Owns Kelly Paddik?
Beth Goobie

Yellow Line
Sylvia Olsen

Zee's Way
Kristin Butcher

Visit www.orcabook.com for more information.

Check out these Orca Currents titles

Check out these Orca Currents titles

Visit www.orcabook.com for more information.